3I-ATLAS: The Convergent

Book Four of the Saga of 3I-ATLAS

By

B.K. Anderson

Copyright © 2026 by B.K. Anderson

All rights reserved.

No part of this book may be reproduced or transmitted in any form or by any means, electronic or mechanical, including photocopying, recording, or by any information storage and retrieval system, without permission in writing from the author, except for brief quotations used in reviews or scholarly works.

This is a work of speculative fiction. Any resemblance to actual persons, events, or phenomena is coincidental and used for narrative purposes.

ISBN# 9798993853178

Printed in the United States of America

Contents

Copyright © 2026 by B.K. Anderson 2

The Saga of 3I-ATLAS 5

Author's Note 6

Prologue — The Convergent 7

CHAPTER ONE — Asian Observation Window 12

CHAPTER TWO — Kael 21

CHAPTER THREE — Shared Attention 30

Transcript-Derived Passage 35

CHAPTER FOUR — Narrowing Geometry 37

CHAPTER FIVE — Interpretation 44

CHAPTER SIX — The Drift 5460

CHAPTER SEVEN — Amplification 60

CHAPTER EIGHT — After the Alignment 66

CHAPTER NINE — Language Tightens 68

CHAPTER TEN — Public Quiet 73

CHAPTER ELEVEN — Human Aftershocks 77

CHAPTER TWELVE — Different Sky 81

Appendix — Institutional Language

(Selected Excerpts) 87

Epilogue — The Silence 89

The Saga of 3I-ATLAS

Book One

Voyage of 3I-ATLAS

Book Two

The Lunar Key

Book Three

The Silence Resonance

Book Four

The Convergent

Author's Note

This book continues the unfolding record of 3I-ATLAS.

As observation deepens, interpretation multiplies. Signals are measured, meanings are debated, and responses emerge—some grounded, some speculative, some deeply human.

The Convergent explores what happens when evidence, belief, and expectation begin to overlap, and when the act of witnessing becomes inseparable from the act of responding.

"What we observe is not nature itself, but nature exposed to our method of questioning."

— Werner Heisenberg

Prologue

The Convergent

No single instrument recorded the moment when the system changed.

There was no flare, no sudden deviation in course, no measurable surge that could be marked with certainty as a beginning. What occurred announced itself only through alignment—through the quiet coincidence of positions that, taken alone, meant little, but together formed a condition that had not existed before.

The object designated **3I-Atlas** continued on its trajectory, inbound and precise. Its speed remained consistent with earlier calculations. Its brightness varied within expected limits. Nothing about its motion demanded alarm.

Yet the geometry around it was no longer incidental.

Sun, Earth, and Jupiter moved into a relationship that narrowed angles and sharpened lines of sight. Phase and opposition reduced uncertainty, stripping away some of the noise that distance and glare had imposed. What had once been glimpsed intermittently could now be held longer in view. Observation windows widened. Data streams lengthened.

Across the planet, attention followed.

Professional observatories adjusted schedules. Independent operators refined their equipment. Networks of small instruments—backyard telescopes, automated trackers, distributed sensors—began to record in parallel. Algorithms collected and sorted the influx, compressing images and curves into forms that could be shared, replicated, and debated.

The object was the same.

The interpretations were not.

In some records, 3I-Atlas remained exactly what it had been declared to be: an interstellar visitor, rare but natural, governed by momentum and mass. In others, it became an anomaly defined by what it did not do, what it failed to resemble, what it resisted categorization as.

Measurements overlapped. Conclusions diverged.

No consensus formed, but something subtler occurred. The act of observation itself intensified. Each new data point altered the questions being asked. Each refinement drew further attention, tightening the feedback between instrument, observer, and object.

Language shifted.

Reports that had once described *tracking* now spoke of *monitoring*. Logs noted *behavior* where earlier entries had recorded only motion. The terminology did not declare intent, yet it implied persistence—an expectation that what was being observed would continue to matter.

And still, 3I-Atlas did not deviate.

It neither accelerated nor corrected its path. It did not signal, flare, or announce itself in any manner that could be isolated as communicative. If it responded at all, it did so only by remaining present—by allowing itself to be seen more clearly as the geometry of the system resolved.

What changed was not the object.

What changed was the structure of awareness around it.

By the time the alignment approached its narrowest window, the object could no longer be considered in isolation. It existed within a closed loop of attention, its passage shaping observation even as observation reshaped meaning. The system—planetary, technological, interpretive—had entered a state in which separation between watcher and watched could no longer be assumed.

Nothing had announced this transition.

There was no signal to mark the crossing.

Only the quiet certainty that from this point forward, observation itself would carry consequences.

CHAPTER ONE Asian Observation

Dawn did not arrive everywhere at once.

Across East Asia, the sky lifted from night in uneven bands of colored indigo over the sea, pale gold above cities, thin rose light spilling across mountains where observatories had kept watch through the dark.

In three different time zones, technicians powered down high-gain imaging runs that had been active since midnight. Arrays cooled. Mirrors settled. Automated trackers completed their final corrections before slipping into standby.

No one declared victory.

No one declared discovery.

At a coastal facility in South Korea, the final frames streamed into a shared repository where timestamps, calibration notes, and environmental readings were automatically attached. A senior operator leaned back from her console and studied the composite without touching a single slider. The object was there — faint, consistent, unremarkable — exactly where the models had placed it.

She wrote only three words in her log: *Position confirmed. Stable.*

Farther south, on a high plateau in Taiwan, a distributed network of smaller instruments had worked in parallel all night. Dozens of modest telescopes, synchronized through cloud software, contributed pieces of the same picture. Individuals the images were ordinary; together they carried weight.

The data did not scream.

It accumulated.

Engineers compared noise profiles across sites. Software stitched frames into a regional mosaic, normalizing for local conditions: humidity, air temperature, minor atmospheric shimmer. The resulting curve did not surprise anyone.

It also did not release them.

Across the region, a quiet rhythm took shape — not a race, but a relay.

In Japan, a national observatory archived its raw files with methodical care, adding them to a growing timeline that now stretched back weeks. Analysts annotated only what could be measured: brightness, phase angle, motion relative to background stars. No speculation accompanied the upload.

In Singapore, researchers correlated their results with satellite-based instruments that observed in a different spectrum. The numbers aligned. That alignment, while reassuring, produced a shared pause — the kind that precedes deeper questions rather than answers.

Private messages moved between institutions.

Not dramatic messages. Not urgent ones. Just notes that began the same way everywhere:

We saw what you saw.

Across borders, dashboards displayed identical plots: smooth lines, predictable variance, no sudden deviations. The object designated 3I-Atlas behaved with the kind of stubborn consistency that made analysts both confident and uneasy.

It was easy to track.

Harder to dismiss.

By midmorning, the first regional summary began to take shape — not as a press statement, but as an internal synthesis circulated among professionals who had watched the same sky from different angles.

The tone was deliberately quiet:

- Geometry favorable.
- Measurements consistent across sites.
- No anomalous motion detected.
- Data quality within expected limits.

No one claimed more than that.

Yet beneath the restraint lay a shared recognition: the alignment window had made this object unusually visible — not just to instruments, but to attention itself.

For the first time, observation was no longer scattered. It was coordinated.

A visualization emerged on a large wall screen in a central data hub: dots representing observatories across East Asia lighting up in sequence as new uploads arrived. The pattern looked less like isolated watching and more like a living network.

No single site owned the record.

The record belonged to all of them.

At one facility, a junior researcher voiced what others were thinking but had not yet said aloud:

"It isn't changing."

Her supervisor did not correct her. Instead, he adjusted the phrasing with professional precision.

"It isn't changing *in a way we can measure.*"

Silence followed — not uncomfortable, but reflective.

Outside the control rooms, ordinary morning life resumed. Trains ran. Markets opened. Children crossed streets on their way to school. None of it paused for an interstellar object passing silently through the solar system.

Inside, however, something subtler had shifted.

The object was no longer merely being tracked. It was held in collective view.

By late afternoon, a regional coordination notes circulated — careful, measured, and entirely free of drama:

Continue parallel monitoring during the remaining alignment window. Share raw frames and calibration metadata. Avoid interpretive conclusions in public summaries.

The language was restrained.

The intent was clear.

They were watching together now.

And they understood that the act of watching — when synchronized — created its own kind of presence.

As the sun set again across East Asia, telescopes began to come online in sequence. Mirrors cooled. Arrays aligned. Software queued fresh runs.

The object remained exactly where it had been predicted to be.

And yet, something about it felt less distant than before.

Not because it had changed.

Because **the way it was being observed had changed.**

Above the curve of Earth, 3I-Atlas continued its silent passage — indifferent to the region that had quietly converged around it.

Below, a network of human attention tightened, patient and disciplined, ready for another night.

No alarms sounded.

No proclamations were made.

Only a shared understanding took root across borders:

The window was open — and they would meet it together.

While observatories across Asia synchronized their instruments and their language, the attention they generated traveled far beyond the region that produced it. Data packets crossed oceans, folded into global networks, and settled quietly into private archives and shared dashboards. The object designated 3I-Atlas was now being held in collective view — yet somewhere beyond all of that coordination, a single observer prepared to meet the same sky in a unique way, alone on a bridge where measurement would remain intimate, restrained, and unshared until he chose otherwise.

CHAPTER Two

Kael Andersson had learned to recognize the difference between a clear night and a useful one.

This was the latter.

The bridge of Celestara was still — not silent, never silent — but steady in a way that invited precision. The curved forward viewport held a deep, unbroken darkness, punctured only by the rising brilliance of Jupiter. Its pale light spilled across consoles and glass, silvering edges without glare.

Kael finished aligning the ship's external array without hurry, fingers moving from memory rather than thought. Calibration lines settled cleanly into their geometry. Systems reported nominal. Nothing argued with him. Nothing rushed him.

He did not look at Jupiter for long.

His attention lay elsewhere.

Celestara, (3I-Atlas), was no longer difficult to locate. The geometry had done its work. What once required patient triangulation and repeated verification now presented itself within a narrower field — its position less ambiguous, its presence harder to dismiss as artifact or coincidence.

From the bridge, Kael brought the telescope array into alignment through the ship's interface and waited for the system to stabilize.

The image resolved slowly on his primary display.

There was nothing dramatic in it. No sudden flare. No sharp alteration in form. The object held its familiar profile, brightness within the margins he had come to expect its motion steady against the background stars.

If he had encountered it without context, he might have dismissed it as merely another faint traveler in a crowded sky.

Yet he did not look away.

The longer he observed, the more he became aware of a subtle pressure — not on the instruments, but on the process itself. Each exposure carried weight. Each adjustment seemed to narrow rather than expand the range of interpretation. The data did not contradict itself, but it resisted simplification.

He captured a sequence and began the slow work of stacking, watching as structure emerged not through enhancement but through persistence. Patterns suggested themselves — not sharply, but with the insistence of something that refused to vanish when corrected for noise.

Kael paused.

He had learned to trust pauses.

The instruments performed within expected limits. Atmospheric distortion — or its spaceborne equivalent — remained minimal.

No alerts flagged the feed. There was nothing in the numbers that demanded alarm.

And yet, the longer the object remained in view, the harder it became to think of it as transient.

He recorded the session and saved the file with deliberate care.

Behind him, the bridge hummed softly — life-support, power regulation, the distant pulse of propulsion in standby. No wind moved here. No trees shifted. Only the quiet breathing of a vessel poised between worlds.

Kael disengaged active tracking and let the system idle, eyes lifting briefly from the screen to the actual sky beyond the glass.

Celestara was invisible to the unaided eye, its presence inferred rather than seen — yet he could not escape the sense that its passage was no longer a solitary event.

It was being watched.

Not only by him.

He powered down the array and left the bridge, moving down the short corridor toward the data bay. The screens there glowed softly in the dim, captured frames waiting with the patience of things that did not require interpretation to exist.

He did not analyze the images immediately.

Experience had taught him that haste introduced distortion — not only in the data, but in the mind of the observer. Instead, he reviewed the session log, verifying timestamps, confirming calibration values, ensuring that nothing in the record could later be dismissed as oversight.

Everything aligned.

That, more than any anomaly, unsettled him.

When he finally brought the images forward for closer examination, he worked without enhancement at first, letting the raw frames speak for themselves. The object maintained its structure across exposures, persistent enough to be named, restrained enough to resist interpretation.

Minor variations appeared where subtle shifts in illumination were expected — slight asymmetries that could be attributed to angle or phase.

And yet.

Kael overlaid the sequences and watched as consistency asserted itself. Patterns did not sharpen so much as hold, refusing to dissolve under correction. He adjusted parameters carefully — removing stars, compensating for drift, aligning frames to the object's motion rather than the background field.

The result was quieter than he had anticipated.

No dramatic revelation emerged. No single frame demanded attention. What remained was something harder to name: a coherence that did not degrade as the data accumulated.

He leaned back and folded his arms.

It was not behaving as an object *should* — not because it violated expectations, but because it conformed too well across conditions that should have introduced greater variance.

The thought came and went without settling, leaving behind a mild tension, like a note that did not resolve.

Kael saved the processed set under a new designation and logged his observations with deliberate neutrality. He chose his language carefully, noting only what could be supported, resisting questions that implied answers he did not yet possess.

Still, the questions formed.

They gathered not at the edges of the data, but at its center — around the persistence of presence, the refusal to fade into statistical insignificance.

He had tracked rare objects before. Interstellar visitors. Anomalies that teased the limits of instruments and models. None of them had left him with the impression that continued observation itself was altering the context in which they were understood.

He shut down the display.

Beyond the viewport, Jupiter burned steadily. The alignment would hold for a while longer, but not indefinitely. Windows narrowed. Conditions shifted. Nothing remained fixed.

Except for the sense that whatever he had been watching was now part of a system that included him.

Kael stood for a moment in the dim glow of the data bay, listening to the soft hum of cooling equipment. He did not feel watched — not in any way he could name — but he could no longer pretend that observation was one-directional.

The thought did not alarm him.
It steadied him.

He opened his notebook and made one final entry for the night, brief and unadorned:

Continued monitoring advised.

Then he closed the book.

Outside, space remained perfectly quiet — and Celestara continued on, unchanged, uninterested, and utterly present.

Chapter Three

Shared Attention

Kael did not send the data out immediately.

He let the files sit through the morning, untouched, while daylight erased the last traces of the night's alignment. Experience had taught him that distance—temporal as much as spatial—was sometimes the only way to see clearly. What remained unchanged after waiting was more likely to matter.

By late afternoon, he reviewed the images again.

They were no different from what he had recorded before. No new structure emerged. No error revealed itself on a second pass. The consistency remained quiet and unyielding. If there was anything unsettling in them, it lay not in what they showed, but in how little they changed when pressed.

Kael selected a subset of the data and prepared it for transmission.

He did not send it broadly. He never did. Instead, he chose two recipients—people whose restraint he trusted, whose questions tended to sharpen rather than scatter. The message he attached was brief, almost perfunctory, noting only conditions, timestamps, and a request for independent verification.

He expected delay.

What he received instead was attention.

The first response arrived within hours, concise and technical. The observer confirmed the geometry, noted similar persistence across exposures, and asked whether Kael had adjusted for object-relative alignment during stacking. Kael replied with details, attaching additional frames.

The second response followed shortly after, longer, more cautious. The data held, the observer agreed, but the lack of degradation across varying conditions was noted as unusual. Not alarming. Unusual.

Kael read both messages twice.

Neither suggested intent. Neither implied anomaly beyond the limits of acceptable variance. And yet, both responses carried the same undertone—a recognition that the object was no longer passing unnoticed through the margins of attention.

By evening, the correspondence had widened without his prompting.

A third observer joined the thread; someone Kael had not contacted directly but had access to the shared exchange. Questions became more precise. Requests for raw frames increased. Time stamps were cross-checked against independent logs.

The language remained careful.

No one claimed discovery.

No one proposed explanation.

Still, the conversation no longer belonged to him.

Kael leaned back from the screen and considered the shift. It was subtle, but unmistakable. The data had crossed a threshold—not of content, but of circulation. What had been private observation had become a shared reference point, a fixed object around which attention began to organize.

He returned to the images once more, this time not as their sole custodian, but as one observer among several.

They had not changed.

That fact now carried a different weight.

Later that night, Kael stepped towards the screen and looked up, not expecting to see anything, knowing better than to search the naked screen for confirmation. The stars offered their familiar indifference. Jupiter burned steadily, unchanged by the quiet exchanges taking place.

Somewhere beyond sight, Celestara continued on its path.

Kael understood then that whatever followed would not unfold in isolation. The object had entered a network of attention that would not easily release it. Each new observer would add context, perspective, and pressure—none of it decisive, all of it cumulative.

He returned to his cabin and closed the correspondence for the night.

The data would persist without him.

That, he suspected, was the point.

Transcript-Derived Passage

As the data circulated, interpretations followed.

Some focused-on geometry and illumination, pointing to phase angle effects and observational bias. Others noted the object's persistence and argued for uncommon—but still natural—behavior within poorly sampled regimes. The discussions remained technical at first, grounded in measurement and method.

Beyond those circles, different readings emerged.

Clips were extracted from longer analyses, stripped of context, and amplified through repetition. Language shifted quickly—from observation to implication, from anomaly to intention. Terms once used cautiously became declarative. Where uncertainty had been acknowledged, certainty was inferred.

None of this altered the object's trajectory.

Celestara continued exactly as before, indifferent to the frameworks imposed upon it. Yet the volume of attention reshaped the event itself. Meaning accumulated faster than evidence. Interpretation outpaced verification.

What had begun as a question of motion and light now carried something less measurable: expectation.

And expectation, once distributed, proved far more difficult to correct than error.

Chapter Four

Narrowing Geometry

The first sign, the window was tightening, did not arrive in the ephemeris.

Kael felt it in work.

The bridge of **Celestara** was the same, lit cleanly by the steady glow of Jupiter beyond the glass. The air was colder, but not unusual . Jupiter still rose bright enough to throw away an image of a faint object. It still held its predicted position with the same indifferent precision. Nothing in the screen declared limitation.

Yet it no longer offered its earlier generosity.

He set the mount and ran the calibration routine twice, not because the first pass failed, but because trust—once broken—

rarely returned without ceremony. It was not equipment he distrusted. It was conditions. Geometry could be merciful, but it could also withdraw without announcement, and the transition between the two often passed unnoticed until the results arrived flawed.

Kael centered the instrument, checked the star shapes at the edges, and adjusted focus by the smallest increments. He watched the first frames come in and noted what they did not show: not new structure, not new behavior, but the beginning of constraint.

The instruments required more attention now. Not longer exposures—those introduced their own errors—but more careful ones. The margin for drift narrowed. The tolerance for atmospheric softness decreased. The same settings that had worked cleanly a week earlier produced faint uncertainty, a slight swell to the stars, and a mild degradation that could be corrected—sometimes.

Sometimes it was not sufficient.

He captured a short run and stacked it quickly, not for revelation, but for confirmation that he still possessed control over the process. The object, Jupiter resolved with its familiar quietness, persistent enough to be named, restrained enough to resist interpretation. Its brightness sat within expected bounds. Its motion remained indifferent.

Kael captured the image.

 Kael saved the raw frames, then the minimal stack, then shut down the enhancement pipeline before it could tempt him.

Outside, the bridge remained quiet. The ship did not seem a lonely place. If anything, it appeared stable, clear, indifferent.

He understood then that narrowing the window was not something the screen would announce.

It was something the process would demand.

He initiated a third run and watched the guiding error climb by a fraction, then settle. He watched it climb again, then settle again. The system was not failing. It was struggling against the mild insistence of diminishing advantage.

And in that insistence, he recognized a threshold: the point at which observation ceased to be simply a matter of time and became a matter of choice.

He could continue to collect frames under these tightening conditions. He could accept the higher variance and compensate in processing. He could chase the last clean data by pushing the system harder, tightening guiding tolerances, increasing the number of exposures.

All of those options were available.

None of them were neutral.

Kael stopped the run early.

It was not a dramatic decision. The sequence had not collapsed. The stars had not turned to streaks. The Jupiter was still present, still stable within the frame. But he could see how the effort to sustain that stability was already altering the character of the data. He could see how easily the record would become something else—a document not of observation, but of insistence.

He powered down the active tracking and let the system idle while he reviewed the session log again, verifying timestamps and calibration values with the same deliberate care he applied when the sky was kinder.

Everything aligned.

That alignment, under narrowing conditions, was never simply a comfort. It was an obligation.

Kael adjusted the instruments more slowly than usual, not because he was tired, but because haste now carried a different consequence. A rushed calculation. A slightly misdated sequence. Each small lapse, once forgivable under generous geometry, now threatened to become the defining flaw in the record.

He Logs were near the workstation, the quiet of the room receiving him without comment. The screens glowed softly. The data waited, indifferent to his awareness of its limits.

Before he slept, he made a single note in his notebook—brief, unadorned, without emphasis:

Window tightening.

Discipline increasing.

Do not compensate into certainty.

Then He closed the book and turned instead to the Log.

.Chapter Five

Anders transmission to Kael

In the quiet background of his own work, Kael was receiving something few others knew about.

Anders — operating as both archivist and translator — had begun to gather what he called *human broadcasts*: the sprawling, unfiltered stream of public reaction, commentary, speculation, and storytelling that had grown around Celestara's name 3I-Atlas.

Anders did not summarize with drama. He curated. He sorted facts from noise, not by declaring what was true, but by showing Kael how meaning was forming in real time. Short clips of analysis sat beside breathless commentary; careful institutional language appeared alongside emotive public claims; technical diagrams were juxtaposed with mythic interpretation.

In his transmissions, Anders made no judgments. Instead, he offered patterns.

Some voices treated Celestara as purely natural — a rare visitor moving without intention. Others framed it as messenger, mirror, or threshold. Still others spoke of portals, timelines, and ascension, projecting spiritual narratives onto a silent object that gave no reply.

Kael read these packets with steady attention. Not to decide who was right, but to understand how humans were responding to uncertainty. What struck him most was not the claims themselves, but the speed with which they traveled. Meaning was spreading faster than measurement.

Anders's quiet collection reminded him that the real event was no longer only in the sky — it was unfolding within human in

Sera Valen enters

Later that same cycle, Sera Valen arrived at the edge of the data bay without announcing herself.

She did not come bearing instruments or files. Her presence was quieter — attentive in a different register than Kael's. Where he measured light and motion, she measured currents of awareness.

Kael glanced up but did not interrupt his work. Sera waited, as she always did, until he looked fully at her.

"The field is accelerating," she said simply.

He did not ask her to clarify. He knew what she meant.

Sera's sensing did not track objects in space. It tracked patterns of attention, emotion, and coherence across the human collective. To her, the weeks surrounding Celestara had not been merely observational — they had been catalytic.

"They are waking faster than we anticipated," she continued, resting one hand lightly on the frame of the console. "Not all of them. Not uniformly. But the baseline has shifted."

Kael considered this without leaning toward belief or disbelief. He simply listened.

Sera described a widening network of intent — people, groups, and communities turning their focus toward healing the Earth rather than exploiting it. In her perception, this was not random activism but a subtle coherence forming beneath ordinary life:

farmers returning to regenerative practices, scientists reconsidering extraction models, artists speaking more openly about interconnection, and children asking diverse kinds of questions.

"It is as if Gaia herself is being remembered," Sera said quietly. "And humans are beginning to feel that memory in their bodies."

She paused, then added something Kael had heard her speak of only once before.

"Others are arriving."

Not ships. Not fleets. Not spectacles in the sky.

What Sera meant by *others* were races and intelligences aligned with planetary restoration — beings who, in her sensing, responded when a world showed signs of self-repair. They were not intervening, she said, but *attending* — offering resonance, insight, or assistance where humans invited it through coherent action.

"They are not coming to save humanity," she clarified, meeting his eyes. "They are coming because humanity is beginning to save itself."

Kael absorbed this in silence. He did not challenge her, nor did he accept her words as fact. Instead, he treated them as another layer of interpretation — meaningful to those who felt it, but not provable by any instrument he possessed.

After a long pause, he asked only one question:

"Is this connected to Celestara?"

Sera did not answer immediately.

"Not as cause," she finally said. "As *mirror*. The object has drawn attention upward, but the awakening is moving outward from within humanity itself."

Kael returned his gaze to the data on the screen — unchanged, precise, indifferent.

Behind him, Sera watched the room rather than the sky, sensing a slow alignment that could not be plotted on any chart.

Between them, observation and intuition held the same quiet space.

The first summaries appeared within days.

They were careful, methodical documents—tables of values, comparative curves, notes on illumination geometry and observational limits. Most agreed on what could be said with confidence: the object's velocity, its persistence across frames, by alignment. Where language remained restrained, the discussion stayed coherent.

Where it did not, divergence followed.

Kael read the exchanges with steady attention, noting how quickly identical data gave rise to incompatible conclusions. Some interpretations emphasized rarity without implication, framing Celestara as a statistical outlier whose behavior fell just beyond familiar categories. Others focused on what was absent—features expected but not observed—and allowed those omissions to carry disproportionate weight.

Outside formal channels, interpretation accelerated.

Short segments of longer analyses circulated independently, detached from their original context. Statements hedged with uncertainty were repeated without qualification. Caution became omission. Omission became implication. The object itself remained unchanged, yet the narrative surrounding it grew increasingly elastic.

Kael recognized the pattern.

He had seen it before—not with celestial objects, but with data that resisted easy explanation. Ambiguity invited projection. Where the evidence declined to resolve, belief moved in to occupy space.

Attempts at correction lagged behind amplification. Clarifications were quieter than claims. Each new interpretation added another layer through which the object would be viewed, rarely removing the layers already in place.

Still, the data held.

Independent confirmations continued to arrive, reinforcing the same restrained conclusions Kael had drawn early on. Nothing in the measurements suggested deviation, signaling, or response. The object neither acknowledged nor resisted the attention being directed toward it.

Yet it was no longer possible to separate observation from expectation.

Kael closed the final report and sat back, aware that the discussion had crossed an invisible line. Interpretation had become an event in itself, one that would continue regardless of what the object did the Great Awaking has started for Gaia.

Celestara moved on.

The meaning attached to it did not.

Chapter Six

The Drift

Kael noticed the change before he could name it.

It did not arrive as error. The data still aligned. resolved cleanly The numbers behaved. If someone had asked him to point to the moment when things shifted, he would not have been able to do so with a timestamp.

The drift did not happen in the sky.

It happened in how people spoke.

He saw it first in a message that assumed too much. The sender was polite, careful even, but the question rested on a conclusion Kael had never made. A phrase he recognized—his own, once—appeared there without its surrounding cautions, stripped down to something firmer, heavier.

He reread the message and felt the familiar tightening behind the eyes.

Compression, not invention.

That was always how it began.

He traced the phrase back through its path: a shared note, a secondary summary, a clipped excerpt paired with an image that was not his. The image was clean enough to convince but unmarked by scale or conditions. The context had evaporated. What remained was confidence.

Kael closed the message without replying.

Correction, he had learned, rarely traveled as far as assumption. Worse, it often lent energy to the very thing it tried to undo. Silence, on the other hand, could be misread—but misreading silence did not alter the record.

The record was still his responsibility.

He opened the archive and pulled up the raw frames again. They had not changed. They never did. The object held its familiar posture against the star field, persistent and unremarkable in the way that demanded discipline from anyone looking too hard.

Nothing in the data asked for meaning.

Meaning was arriving anyway.

He watched how language shifted as it moved outward. "Tracking" became "monitoring." "Monitoring" became "attention." Attention acquired tone, and tone suggested intent. The object's refusal to do anything unusual was recast as restraint, then patience, then—by some—design.

Kael felt no anger at this.

He recognized it.

Humans did not tolerate unresolved things well. When observation reached its limit, interpretation rushed in to close the gap. The absence of signal was treated as signal itself. Silence became a surface onto which expectation could be projected.

He returned to his own work.

Each night's session was logged with the same care as before. He resisted invitations to summarize, to interpret, to frame. He provided raw frames when asked, timestamps intact, calibration notes unedited. He refused to supply "the clearest image," because clarity did not exist outside conditions.

There were only moments, and those moments were passing.

The drift continued without him.

He saw his words again, altered slightly, sharpened where he had softened them. He saw his caution repurposed as authority. None of it reflected what he had actually done, but all of it felt inevitable once attention reached a certain density.

Celestara itself remained indifferent.

That, more than anything, steadied him.

If the object had changed—if it had flared, deviated, responded—then the narratives forming around it might have found purchase in fact. But it did not. It simply passed through the system that had chosen to focus on it.

The drift belonged to them.

Later that night, Kael left the data bay and returned to the bridge of **Celestara**.

He stood before the viewport, not expecting to see anything, knowing better than to search the naked darkness for confirmation. The stars offered their familiar indifference. Jupiter burned steadily, unchanged by the quiet exchanges taking place across vast distances.

Somewhere beyond sight, **Celestara** continued on its path.

Kael understood then that whatever followed would not unfold in isolation. The object had entered a network of attention that would not easily release it. Each new observer would add context, perspective, and pressure — none of it decisive, all of it cumulative.

He returned to his cabin and closed the correspondence for the night.

The data would persist without him.

That, he suspected, was the point.

Chapter Seven

Amplification

Kael noticed the change the way one notices a room growing louder without anyone raising their voice.

There was no announcement, no single moment he could point to and say *here*. No press release that marked a boundary. What shifted did so through repetition—small phrases repeated often enough that they began to sound permanent. Words that had once leaned carefully on *if* and *may* lost their balance and stood upright on their own.

He saw it first at the edges.

A graph appeared stripped of its margin notes. A conditional sentence quoted without its second half. Timelines smoothed until the irregularities vanished, replaced by the comfort of sequence. The language had not changed much, but its posture had. It no longer waited.

Kael did not feel alarm at first. Only a tightening—subtle, like a muscle adjusting to a long-held position. He had spent years of training observation to know that meaning often migrated faster than facts. Data stayed put. Interpretation wandered.

He reads more slowly now.

Each article carried echoes of earlier ones, phrases passed along intact, as if repetition itself had become evidence. The qualifiers were still present in the original papers. He knew that. He had written some of them himself. But the copies that traveled outward shed those cautions the way heat sheds detail at a distance.

He wondered when he had crossed from contributor to reference.

It was unsettling to see his words reflected back to him without their context, sharpened into shapes he had not intended. Not wrong, exactly—but more certain than he felt. As though the hesitation he had built into them had been edited out by time.

Late that night, Kael leaned back from his desk and let his eyes rest on the primary viewing screen.

Jupiter filled the frame — vast, luminous, and unhurried, its bands of light moving in slow, patient rhythm far beyond the hull of **Celestara**. The planet did not press for interpretation. It simply endured.

For a moment, Kael stopped thinking about data, commentary, or the widening human narratives around 3I-Atlas. Instead, he allowed his attention to settle on that distant presence.

He remembered, quietly, that his role had never been only observational. In earlier cycles, he had been asked — not commanded — by the **Galactic Council** to perform calibrated releases of energy toward Earth during specific alignments, designed to support what they called *human code upgrades*.

He had never spoken of this publicly, and he did not treat it as a claim to be proven. To him, it was simply part of the work of his station: subtle, timing-dependent, and coordinated with larger cosmic systems he could not fully explain.

Looking at Jupiter now, he understood something more clearly than before.

The amplification unfolding across Earth was not driven by any single object — not by Celestara, not by him, not even by the Council. It was being carried forward by human attention itself.

If his earlier energy releases had mattered at all, they had done so only as gentle catalysts — openings, not causes.

Kael turned away from the screen, satisfied with that restraint.

Outside the viewport, Jupiter glowed steadily in the dark.

Inside **Celestara**, the room settled into silence — not empty but poised — as the larger system continued to move without drama.

Because amplification did not require falsity. It only requires momentum. And momentum, once established, was difficult to interrupt without appearing to oppose it.

He closed his notebook and sat in the dim.

If the moment demanded anything of him, he suspected it was patience. The willingness to let uncertainty remain intact a little longer. To resist the pull toward resolution simply because others were tired of waiting.

Kael knew this phase well.

It was not discovery that unsettled institutions. It was ambiguity that lingered.

Kael returned to his desk and opened the raw data again.

He trusted that more than the noise. Trusted that what mattered would not need to be shouted into existence.

Somewhere ahead, the trajectory would narrow. Or it would not. Either way, he would be there to see it—not amplified, not reduced—only observed.

And for now, that would have to be enough.

Chapter Eight

After the Alignment

Kael noticed it was not the absence of activity—data continued to arrive, instruments still recorded, and analysts remained at their desks—but the tone had changed. The urgency that once pressed against every update had eased, replaced by something more measured. Observation no longer felt like pursuit. It felt like attendance.

The alignment had passed, but its effects lingered. Geometry had done its work and then withdrawn, leaving behind a clarity that did not demand explanation. The object designated 3I-Atlas remained consistent in brightness and motion. Nothing in its trajectory suggested intention or deviation. And yet, Kael found himself reading the reports more slowly now, as if speed itself had become unnecessary.

Interpretation, he noticed, had begun to spread.

The same data sets produced different conclusions depending on who held them. Some voices leaned toward confidence, others toward caution. A few began to speculate beyond what the measurements supported, filling the remaining uncertainty with expectation. Kael did not join them. He recorded what could be recorded and let the rest remain unshaped.

He understood, more clearly than before, that attention alters tone. Jupiter had not changed. The observers had.

And that, he suspected, was where the real convergence had begun.

Chapter Nine

Language Tightens

Official statements arrived later than expected.

They were brief, carefully phrased, and notably uniform. Terms like *consistent, within expected variance*, and *no confirmed anomaly* appeared with increasing frequency. Nothing was denied outright, but nothing was invited either. The language had narrowed, not to obscure, but to contain.

Kael read each release without annotation. He recognized the pattern. Institutions do not speak until they must, and when they do, they choose words that can hold multiple futures at once.

Internally, the discussions continued. Parameters were refined. Thresholds adjusted. Observation windows recalculated. None of them suggested crisis. None of them suggested closure. It was maintenance—of systems, of credibility, of patience.

Kael felt no frustration at the restraint. If anything, it reassured him. Excess certainty would have unsettled him far more than silence.

He noted how often the word *monitoring* appeared. Not studying. Not investigating. Monitoring implied coexistence.

That distinction mattered.

Later that evening, after the last official statements had been filed and archived, Kael returned to the bridge of **Celestara** and opened a quiet channel.

"Sera," he said simply. "When you have a moment."

She arrived without haste, moving into the dim light beside him as if the request had been expected. For a time, neither spoke. Jupiter glowed steadily on the main screen; the instruments hummed at low power.

At last Kael gestured toward the data stream of human commentary scrolling faintly along a secondary display — not images of the sky, but the *chatter* surrounding it: public reactions, quiet anxieties, bursts of inspiration, and threads of renewed care for Gaia.

"Give me your assessment," he said. "Not of the object — of the field beneath it."

Sera closed her eyes briefly, not to withdraw but to attune. When she spoke, her voice was calm, grounded, and without drama.

"Gaia is steadier than she was," she said. "Not healed — but remembering. The human current is uneven, yet stronger. There is more coherence in small places than there was before: communities restoring land, children asking different questions, interconnection without apology."

She paused, sensing rather than measuring.

"The chatter is not louder. It is *clearer*. Fear still moves through it, but it is less dominant. Curiosity is replacing it in many channels."

Kael listened without interrupting.

"And the others?" he asked quietly.

Sera did not frame this as spectacle.

"They are present, but not intervening," she replied. "Attending where coherence invites it. Supporting, not directing. Waiting, not arriving."

Kael considered this, then nodded once.

"So, the shift is human, not imposed."

"Yes," Sera said. "And that is why it may endure.

They stood together in silence for a long moment — instrument light soft on metal, Jupiter turning slowly beyond the viewport — until Kael finally spoke again.

"Thank you."

Sera inclined her head and withdrew as quietly as she had come, leaving the bridge to its steady hum.

Kael returned his attention to the official summaries, seeing them now not as limits, but as a surface beneath which something deeper was moving.

CHAPTER TEN Public Quiet

The expected reaction never arrived.

There was no sustained panic, no singular narrative that seized the public imagination. Interest spiked, then diffused. Some watched closely for signs that never came. Others lost attention altogether. The absence of spectacle left nothing to rally around.

Kael observed this with mild surprise. Humanity was accustomed to crescendo—to moments that announced themselves loudly. What unfolded instead was something subtler: a collective hesitation. Conversations paused. Arguments softened. Curiosity lingered without direction.

Information circulated, but it did not cohere. Without a story to inhabit, speculation scattered. The object remained distant, quiet, resistant to dramatization.

Kael thought of silence not as emptiness, but as a surface that reflected whatever approached it. Some saw reassurance. Others saw unease. Most simply moved on.

He wrote in his notes: *Lack of narrative is itself a stabilizing force.*

Kael returned to the data again and again, not searching for revelation, but for consistency.

The Celestara continued its passage, indifferent to attention. Measurements aligned across instruments and methodologies. No signal announced itself. No threshold was crossed. What had once felt like approach now felt like passage.

He considered his role carefully. He was not an interpreter, not a messenger, not a voice meant to persuade. He was a witness and witnessing required discipline.

To observe without projecting.

To record without concluding.

To allow uncertainty to remain intact.

Kael realized that restraint had become the most accurate response available. Anything more would distort what little clarity had been gained.

The systems around him adjusted accordingly. Schedules normalized. Language softened further. Celestara receded—not in distance, but in urgency.

And Kael found that he was grateful for that.

Eventually, even the questions grew quieter.

There came a point when additional observation yielded no new distinctions. Variance flattened. Anomalies resolved into background. Instruments did not fail, they simply stopped discovering.

Kael understood what that meant.

Some phenomena do not conclude. They settle.

The object designated 3I-Atlas had not departed, nor had it revealed anything final. It had entered a state of coherence with the systems observing it, becoming part of the environment rather than a subject within it.

He closed his final session without ceremony.

The silence that followed was not abrupt. It arrived gradually, like a room dimming as evening deepened. There was relief in it. A sense that nothing further was required.

Kael recorded one final line:

Observation complete does not mean understanding complete.

Then he let the file rest.

CHAPTER ELEVEN Human Aftershocks

The Local Scientist

Dr. Marisol Ortega had not planned to be awake at three in the morning.

Her lab was quiet in the way that scientific spaces become quiet at night — lights dimmed, instruments humming softly, screens glowing with patient graphs that never slept.

For weeks she had followed the data on 3I-ATLAS with professional detachment. She had run models, checked assumptions, and written careful memos that avoided speculation. Her job was to keep interpretation disciplined.

Still, she watched.

Not only the object — but the way people responded to it.

On the night the alignment finally receded, she sat alone at her workstation and replayed a montage of human reaction she had compiled for her own private use:

students asking new questions, farmers experimenting with soil restoration, community groups organizing river cleanups, artists releasing work that spoke openly of interconnection.

None of this appeared in her official reports.

Yet it stayed with her more than the curves on her screen.

She pulled up one last dataset — not astronomical, but ecological. Carbon capture readings from small local projects; water quality tests from community-led cleanups; biodiversity counts from regenerating land. They were modest numbers.

Not world-saving.

Not dramatic.

But they were real.

Marisol leaned back in her chair and felt something shift that no instrument could measure: a subtle reorientation in how she understood her work.

She had entered science to *understand the world.*

She was beginning to see that understanding also meant *participating in its care.*

Before shutting down her computer, she typed one sentence into her personal notebook — not the lab log:

"If attention can move toward the stars, it can also return to the ground."

She powered down the lights and stepped out into the cool night.

Above her, the sky was ordinary.

No signs, no messages, no miracles.

Yet she walked home with a steadier sense of purpose than she had felt in years.

Not because of what 3I-ATLAS had done.

Because of what humans were beginning to do.

"I learned that attention is a form of participation."

She did not send this to anyone.

She did not post it.

She closed the notebook and returned to her studies.

Years later, when she would design bridges, she would remember the weeks of 3I-ATLAS — not for what it had revealed in the sky, but for what it had revealed in herself:

That some things are not meant to be captured, only witnessed.

"And that witnessing, done carefully, changes the witness."

CHAPTER TWELVE — Different Horizon

Celestara route was unchanged.

The light was softer than it had been weeks earlier — not dimmer, but less urgent, as if Jupiter's glow had settled into a steady companion rather than a spotlight.

Kael moved through the bridge without hurrying.

In the bridge viewport **of Celestara, Jupiter filled the distance monitor — vast, luminous, and unhurried.** Its slow bands of light turned with a patience that needed no interpretation.

He watched without measuring.

He listened without recording. He stood at the bridge of **Celestara**, eyes resting on the distant glow of Jupiter.

He was not human, yet he understood humans more deeply than before.

He was not separate from them, yet he remained what he had always been —

a guardian moving in harmony with the larger cosmos.

What had shifted was not his nature, but his knowing.

He no longer needed perfect certainty.

He had learned to hold space for mystery.

Celestara hummed quietly around him, steady and alive.

And in that stillness, Kael felt something new — not doubt, not urgency, but **deep composure.**

The mission had not ended.

It had matured.

"To watch well is enough."

So, he closed the book and dimmed the lights.

Beyond the viewport, Jupiter turned slowly in the dark. Farther still, Celestara continued its silent passage.

Kael stepped back into the center of the bridge and let his gaze widen — not toward any single object, but toward the whole field of space.

For the first time, he did **not** feel like someone standing apart from the cosmos.

He felt **inside it.**

Not special.

Significant.

Simply here.

He remained standing there for a long time.

Gradually, something subtle began to occur — not in the sky, but in the room itself.

The hum of systems softened.

The background data streams slowed.

The constant low-level chatter of observation quieted.

Not because instruments failed.

Not because attention vanished.

But because nothing **demanded response anymore.**

Kael noticed it before he named it.

A deep stillness, spreading not as absence — but as coherence.

He glanced at the primary display.

The usual streams of incoming commentary, analysis, and reaction had thinned to a trickle.

Not panic.

Not exhaustion.

Simply… quiet.

He touched the console once, lightly.

No alarms.

No requests.

No new directives.

For the first time since the alignment, there was **nothing he needed to prepare for.**

He looked again through the viewport.

The stars held their distances.

Jupiter glowed with calm permanence.

And in that moment, Kael understood something that would carry him forward into what came next:

Silence was not emptiness.

Silence was alignment.

He powered down the final auxiliary screen.

The bridge settled.

Celestara continued on.

And Kael felt — not finished — but **centered at the threshold of something larger.**

He whispered to himself:

"Next comes the Great Silence."

The lights dimmed completely.

Appendix

Institutional Language

The following phrases appear in official communications, internal memoranda, and public briefings during the final observation window. They are presented without commentary.

"Within expected variance."

"No anomalous risk identified at this time."

"Data under continued review."

"Instrument sensitivity limits reached."

"Correlation does not imply causation."

"Operational posture unchanged."

"Public reassurance advised."

"Further clarification pending."

"Event considered non-persistent."

"Observation complete."

In later documents, the language simplifies.

"Systems nominal."

"No further action required."

The absence of new terminology is notable.

Epilogue

The Silence

Kael noticed the silence before anyone named it.

It was not the absence of sound, or of data, or even of attention.

It was the absence of *pressure*.

Nothing leaned forward anymore.

The channels stayed open.

The instruments remained powered.

But nothing insisted on being interpreted.

He read the last summaries twice. They were careful. Accurate.

They did not contradict one another.

They did not add anything.

Outside, the night sky looked the same as it always had.

Stars held their distances.

The object was where the models said it would be.

Still, something had changed.

Not in the sky —

but in the waiting.

Kael closed the file and did not replace it with another.

For the first time since the alignment, there was nothing he needed to prepare for.

The silence did not feel empty.

It felt complete.

He suspected it would not last.

Nothing ever does.

But it was enough to know that, for a moment,

the universe was not asking to be understood.

Only witnessed.

"next comes the Great Silence"

www.ingramcontent.com/pod-product-compliance
Lightning Source LLC
LaVergne TN
LVHW041625070526
838199LV00052B/3250